About this book

Arnhem Land belongs to the Aboriginal people who have lived there for more than 40,000 years. There are many different tribes and language groups throughout Arnhem Land, but at Gunbalanya, where this book is set, the main language spoken is Kunwinjku (pronounced "goon – win – goo").

I visited Arnhem Land in 1996 and 1997 as a guest of the Gunbalanya Community School, with my friend and fellow author Liz Honey. Together we worked with staff and students of the school to produce poems, plays, puppets and paintings. This book is based on a story the Upper Primary students made about their lives called "We Love Gunbalanya".

Thanks to Rowan, Andrew, Anita, Bill and Maree for their friendship and help, Esther Djayhgurrnga, Julie Narndal, Moses Mirrawana, Donald Gumurdul and Jacob Nayinggul for their advice, and the children for sharing their stories.

The seasons and how to pronounce their names

Kudjewk (goo – jawk): monsoon season (December to March).

Bangkerreng (bung – ge – reng): harvest time (March to May).

Yekke (yek – ge): cool weather season (May to June).

Wurrkeng (whirr (rr is rolled) – geng): early dry season (June to August).

Kurrung (gurr (rr is rolled) – roong): hot, dry season (August to October).

Kurnumeleng (goo – noo – meleng): pre-monsoon season (October to December).

Ernie Dances to the Didgeridoo

For the children of Gunbalanya

Alison Lester

HOUGHTON MIFFLIN COMPANY BOSTON

Walter Lorraine Books

Ernie is going to live in Arnhem Land for a year.

Ernie waves goodbye to Rosie, Frank, Tessa, Nicky, Clive and Celeste, and promises to write them a letter for each of the six Arnhem Land seasons.

He flies above the desert for hours

His parents are working at a hospital there.

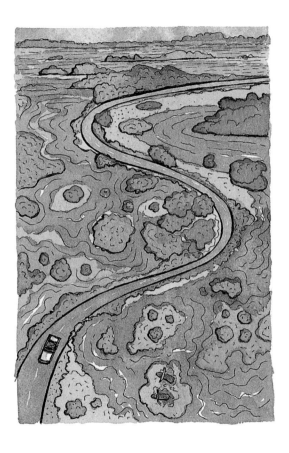

and lands in Darwin.
It's hot.

He travels over
the floodplains,

crosses the
East Alligator River,

and arrives at his new home.

Dear Clive, it's Kudjewk now, the monsoon season.

Sammi surfs in
the puddles.

Christine slides in
the mud.

Ernie catches frogs.

It rains every day but I am having a good time.

Joseph plays football.

Patrick spears a barramundi.

And Jenna rides her bike in the rain.

But Tammy and her baby brother watch a goanna
floating on the floodwaters.

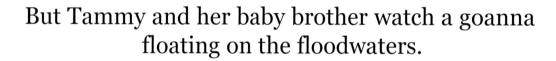

Dear Frank, it's Bangkerreng, harvest time.

Christine plays tin-tin.

Sammi jumps into
the waterfall.

Ernie sneaks up on
the buffalo.

It has stopped raining and the sun shines every day.

Patrick collects
goose eggs.

Joseph does backflips
off the coconut tree.

And Tammy gets
chased by a crocodile.

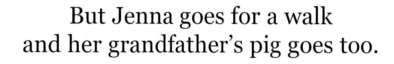

But Jenna goes for a walk
and her grandfather's pig goes too.

Dear Nicky, it's Yekke now, cool weather time.

Patrick gets
painted with the
Crocodile Dreaming.

Joseph and his
uncle collect bark
for painting.

Christine digs for yams

The waterlilies are flowering and they smell beautiful.

Ernie learns to make
a spear.

Jenna dances at
the disco.

And Tammy goes for
sugar bag.

But Sammi is frightened by the Mimi stilt dancers.

Dear Celeste, it's Wurrkeng, the early dry season.

Tammy catches a
file snake.

Ernie goes fishing.

Joseph takes his sister
for a walk.

The grass is yellow and there are lots of mosquitoes.

Jenna's mother teaches
her to weave pandanus.

Sammi plays tin-trucks.

And Christine learns
the yam dance.

But Patrick's grandfather tells him about
the Creation Mother.

Dear Rosie, Kurrung is here, the hot dry season.

Jenna catches a crab
at the beach.

Patrick and his little
sisters eat icypoles.

Ernie collects green
plums with Old Daisy.

There is hardly any water in the billabong.

Tammy digs up a
long-necked turtle.

Christine has her
ears inspected.

And Sammi's uncle tells
him a Dreamtime story
about the moon.

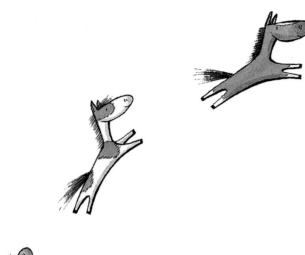

But Joseph surprises a thirsty horse under his house.

Dear Tessa, it's Kurnumeleng, the pre-monsoon season.

Patrick is a horse in the school play.

Tammy is a butterfly.

Sammi is a frog.

It's very humid and there are thunderstorms every day.

Ernie is a
frill-necked lizard.

Jenna is a corella.

And Joseph is
Kinga, the crocodile.

But Christine rings the bell on Santa's truck.

Dear Ernie, thank you for your letters.

Celeste is a stilt dancer.

Clive wears body paint.

djenj (jeng) fish

kunj (goo-ng) kangaroo

narmarnkol (nar-mun -gol)

barramundi.

bo bo - goodbye

Tessa teaches us some
Kunwinjku words.

We are doing special Arnhem Land activities at school.

Nicky does a bark
painting of her
guinea pig.

Rosie makes damper.

And Frank is a hunter
and his dog Roger
is a dingo.

But we wonder what you are doing Ernie?

Meanings and explanations

Arnhem Land: Australia's largest Aboriginal reserve, east of Darwin, in the Northern Territory.

Barramundi: large fish found in the north of Australia.

Billabong: a lake which reconnects with a river in flood times.

Corella: small cockatoo.

Creation Mother: part of a Dreamtime story.
She cast out names, languages, tribes, clans, etc, as she travelled the land.

Damper: bread made from flour and water and cooked in hot sand covered with hot coals.

Darwin: capital city of the Northern Territory.

Dingo: wild dog of Australia.

Dreamtime stories: spiritual beliefs on how the land was formed; creation stories.

File snake: rough-skinned aquatic snake found in Arnhem Land.

Floodplains: plains bordering a river. The plains flood each wet season.

Goanna: large carniverous lizard.

Icypole: flavored ice on a stick.

Kinga: Kunwinjku word for crocodile.

Kunwinjku (goon – win – goo): name of the people and language of Gunbalanya.

Mimi stilt dancers: dance group that performs Dreamtime stories of Mimi spirits.

Pandanus: palm-like tree. Its leaves are used for weaving.

Sugar bag: bush honey from a native bee.

Tin-tin: game played by Aboriginal children. The aim is to knock down tin cans stacked in a pyramid.

Tin trucks: toy truck made by Aboriginal children.
They use wire and a powdered milk tin to make the trucks.

Yam dance: Kunwinjku dance of celebration.

This book was created with the help and approval of the Gunbalanya School Council

Walter Lorraine Books

Copyright © 2000 by Alison Lester
First American edition 2001
Originally published in Australia by
Hodder Headline Australia Pty Limited

Library of Congress Cataloguing-in-Publication Data

Lester, Alison
    Ernie dances to the didgeridoo / by Alison Lester.
        p.   cm.
    Summary: When Ernie leaves the city and goes to live in Arnhem
Land, he sends letters to his old classmates describing the activities of his new friends.
    ISBN 0-618-10442-9
    1. Arnhem Land (N.T.)--Juvenile fiction. [1. Arnhem Land(N.T.)--Fiction. 2.
    Australian aborigines--Fiction. 3. Letters--Fiction. 4. Australia--Fiction] I. Title.
PZ7.L56284 Er   2001
[E]--dc21   00-040680

Printed in China
10 9 8 7 6 5 4 3 2 1